Spring Break-Up

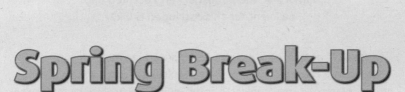

Spring Break-Up

Adapted by Jane Mason and Sara Hines Stephens
Based on teleplays Written by Dan Schneider

Based on the television series "Zoey 101" created by Dan Schneider

SCHOLASTIC INC.

New York   Toronto   London   Auckland   Sydney
Mexico City   New Delhi   Hong Kong   Buenos Aires

No part of this work may be reproduced in whole or in part,
stored in a retrieval system, or transmitted in any form or by any
means, electronic, mechanical, photocopying, recording, or otherwise,
without written permission of the publisher. For information regarding
permission, write to Scholastic Inc., Attention: Permissions
Department, 557 Broadway, New York, NY 10012.

ISBN 0-439-84872-5

Published by Scholastic Inc.

12 11 10 9 8 7 6 5 4 3 2 1   6 7 8 9 10/0

Printed in the U.S.A.

First printing, September 2006

Spring Break-Up

Seize the Day

Zoey Brooks walked across the green lawn to her favorite place on the Pacific Coast Academy campus. Sitting down under a shady tree, she pulled her red laptop with the pear logo on its cover out of her bag. She had a lot of packing to do for spring break but she wanted to send an overdue e-mail to her grandparents before she forgot.

Zoey looked out at the blue Pacific and smiled. PCA was definitely the best school she'd gone to, hands down.

Opening her laptop, Zoey began to type.

Dear Grandma and Grandpa,

PCA has been great this semester. On my last report card, I got all A's and one B. But the good news is the B was at the bottom, so if you hold your thumb over it, it looks just like all A's.

Anyway, I'm so excited 'cause next week is spring break — and you'll never guess where I'm going. You know that guy Logan I told you about? Well, he invited me and Dustin and all my friends to his house in Santa Barbara. His dad's this major TV and movie producer, so the place is supposed to be amazing.

Well, I better go pack. Oh, and lemme know if that thing on Grandpa's neck went away. Hope so.

Love, Zoey

Zoey looked over the letter, then added a little smiley face next to her name before hitting SEND. Mission accomplished. Now she could get down to the nitty-gritty of getting ready for the best vacation ever!

Across campus, Chase Matthews and Michael Barrett were in their dorm room, loading up their suitcases.

"Man, I am so psyched for spring break," Chase said as he tossed a stack of T-shirts into his bag. It had been a l-o-n-g semester, and a week of chillin' with his friends was just what he needed.

"You and me both," Michael agreed. "I need to destress." He looked thoughtful. "Hey, how many pairs of underwear you think I should pack?" he asked as he tossed a pair of surf shorts into his bag.

Chase shook his head, making his dark, unruly curls bob. He couldn't be serious. "Y'know, I really don't feel qualified to help you with your underwear math," he replied, looking a little weirded out.

But Michael was taking the matter seriously. He tapped a finger on his chin. "Let's see. . . . We're gonna be at Logan's house for six days, and I like to change at least once . . ."

Chase eyed a bottle of cologne on his dresser. He wanted to slip it into his bag but didn't want Michael to see. Luckily Michael was totally engrossed in his underwear math, ticking off the days on his fingers. Out of the corner of his eye, Chase made sure his roomie wasn't looking, then grabbed the cologne off his dresser and shoved it under some clothes in his bag.

Just as he covered it up, Michael turned in Chase's direction. He dropped the boxers he was holding. "Hey, what'd you just pack in your suitcase?" he asked, raising an eyebrow.

"Nothin'," Chase replied. Trying to act casual, he stepped in front of his bag, in case Michael decided to see for himself.

"Yeah, ya did," Michael replied evenly. "What was it?" He tried to dodge right past his friend, but Chase blocked him. He dodged again, but Chase raised his eyebrows and smiled. He wasn't giving anything up — if he could help it.

"Fine," Michael said with a shrug. "Don't lemme see." He casually turned toward his own half-packed bag. But as soon as Chase had turned his back, he spun around fast and went straight for the mystery item. A second later he was holding a fancy glass bottle of men's cologne. "Ha!" he said victoriously.

"Okay." Chase was resigned. He was going to take some flack from his best friend. At least it wasn't Logan. . . . "Gimme that," he said, hoping to nip the conversation in the bud.

Michael laughed. "Ah, cologne?" Michael teased, waving the bottle in the air. He was actually a little surprised. He didn't have Chase pegged as a cologne kind of guy.

"No. It's medicine," Chase babbled, thinking fast. "For . . . pimples." Ugh. How lame was that?

"Well, you must have some pretty sweet-smelling pimples," Michael said, smirking and taking a whiff. Who did Chase think he was kidding?

Chase grabbed the bottle. "A pimple can't smell

4

nice?" he asked accusingly as he tucked the bottle back into his bag.

Michael planted his hands on his hips and gave Chase the eye. "I think you wanna smell nice for a certain young lady who goes by the name of Zo-o-oey," he said, stretching out Zoey's name for effect.

"Maybe I wanna smell nice for you — ever think of that?" Chase asked sarcastically. He turned and got back to his packing, hoping that would shut Michael up. Except, of course, it didn't.

"You know what you ought to do on this spring break trip?" Michael asked.

"What should I do?" Chase asked, not sure he really wanted Michael's opinion on the matter.

"Tell Zoey you love her," Michael announced with a sigh.

Chase waved a hand at his friend. "Man, go do your underwear math," he said, irritated.

Michael didn't give up. "It's the perfect time, man! Spring break, Santa Barbara, right by the beach." His voice got a faraway sound and he gestured with his arms as if he were setting the perfect stage. "Very romantic," he finished, raising an eyebrow and hoping Chase would get the message.

"So?" Chase asked.

Ugh. How thick was he? "So, it's the perfect time for you to tell Zoey you love her," Michael repeated.

Chase dropped some clothes into his suitcase and took several steps toward Michael. "Will you stop saying that so loud?" he said, looking over his shoulder to make sure no one was eavesdropping out in the hall.

"Why?" Michael asked, not sure what the big deal was.

"I don't want people to know, okay?" Chase said, looking sheepish. His feelings for Zoey were private.

Michael rolled his eyes. Was he serious? "Dude, everyone on planet Earth knows you love Zoey," he said emphatically. "The people on *Neptune* know it. Yeah, they're up there right now on Neptune, saying, 'Hey, did you know that Chase loves Zoey?'" Michael spoke in perfect alien, turning his head like some kind of space creature. "'Why, yes, I do. The whole galaxy knows,'" Michael finished.

Chase waved his friend off. "You talk so much," he said, getting back to his packing.

But Michael wasn't backing off. He wasn't trying to be mean or anything, he was just tired of watching Chase torment himself over Zoey. Telling her how he felt seemed like the best choice. "Look, the only person who doesn't know you love Zoey is Zoey, so why don't you just tell her already?" he asked reasonably.

Chase looked at his friend. Didn't Michael know he'd thought about that a thousand times? It was kinda hard to explain. "Because I don't want Zoey to know that I love . . ."

At that exact moment Logan Reese, their third roommate, strolled into the room, still wet from the shower and with a bright orange towel slung over his shoulders. Logan was not exactly the kind of person you wanted to confide in.

". . . brussels sprouts," Chase finished lamely. It was a stupid choice of words, but at least he caught himself before he said "Zoey."

"You love brussels sprouts?" Logan echoed, giving Chase a strange look.

"Yeah." Chase nodded. "They're, like, my favorite vegetable. That a problem?" he asked, looking a little offended.

"No," Logan said with a shrug. Whatever.

Just then another guy in the dorm walked by the door and peeked his head in. "Hey, Reese," he called to Logan. "You left your shampoo in the shower."

"And you couldn't bring it to me?" Logan shouted

after him, disgusted. Was it so hard to carry a bottle of shampoo to his room?

"Nope." The voice was already halfway down the hall.

Logan rolled his eyes and headed back to the bathroom. "Back in a sec," he said as he disappeared out the door.

As soon as he was gone, Chase turned to Michael. "Will you quit talking about me and Zoey in front of Logan?" he begged.

"If you tell her you love her," Michael shot back.

"No!" Chase insisted.

"Gimme one good reason."

"All right, you want a reason? I'll give you a reason," Chase said. "What if I tell Zoey I love her, and she doesn't love me back?" There, he'd said it. His worst nightmare was out. "That'll make things so awkward between us, it could wreck our friendship forever."

Michael had to admit that Chase had a point. But why was he assuming the worst? It was quite possible that Zoey was crazy about him, too. "But if she does love you back, then she'll become your girlfriend and you'll be 'Happy Chase' forever."

Chase shook his head. He longed to be Happy Chase, to have Zoey as a girlfriend. But being her friend was a lot better than weirdness. "It's not worth the risk." He turned back to his suitcase.

"Life is *about* taking risks," Michael insisted, holding his arms out to Chase in a plea. "Remember that saying we learned in Latin? *Carpe doom?* Seize the day!"

"Uh, it's *carpe diem*," Chase enunciated.

Michael looked confused. "Then what's *carpe doom*?" he asked.

"Stupid," Chase said flatly.

"Oh, yeah," Michael said sheepishly.

Gender Defenders

Zoey stood in PCA's main drive, feeling great — and looking great, too, in a wild, hot-pink T-shirt, short jean mini, and dangly hoop earrings. All around her, students were loaded down with bags, surfboards, and other necessary vacation items. Spring break was officially starting! Or officially about to, at least. The whole gang was waiting to leave for Logan's house — Chase; Michael; Logan; her little brother, Dustin; her new roommate, Lola Martinez; PCA's resident genius, Quinn Pensky; and Zoey's best friend, Nicole Bristow. Hey, wait, where was Nicole?

"How are we all gonna fit in one car?" Dustin asked. It was a good question, since there were eight of them.

"Don't worry about it," Logan said knowingly. He did a quick count of his waiting friends. Someone was missing . . . one of the girls. "Hey, where's Nicole?" he asked, annoyed. He wanted all his friends to be there when their ride showed up. He was pretty sure it was going to make an impression, and impressions were what life was all about. "I told everyone to be here on time."

Zoey checked her cell for messages and shrugged. She had no idea where Nicole was at the moment but knew she'd be here. Who would miss her ride to the vacation of a lifetime? "Relax, here she comes," she said, nodding toward the walkway behind Logan.

Nicole had just appeared from the other side of a perfectly trimmed hedge, smiling and looking great in a baby-blue and green seersucker halter dress. "C'mon . . . just a little farther." She clapped her hands together encouragingly. "No pain, no gain . . ." she babbled.

Behind her, a pair of younger boys was dragging Nicole's giant duffel bag. They barely cleared the hedge, causing the giant bag to scrape against the branches. "Careful!" Nicole scolded as she stepped up to the curb with the rest of her friends.

The boys dropped the bag to the ground, falling on top of it, exhausted.

"Thanks, guys. You can go now," Nicole dismissed the underclassmen cheerfully while she dug around for something in her red and white Hawaiian-print bag.

One of the kids leaped to his feet. "Hey, you said you'd give each of us ten bucks!" he protested loudly.

Nicole wrinkled her nose at the idea. "I was kidding," she said with a perky smile. "Run along," she added.

One of the kids started toward her in a huff, but the other pulled him back. Rolling their eyes, they walked off.

Logan laughed to himself as the two kids walked away. Suckers! But before they were out of view, he remembered that he had some news for his friends.

"So, guys . . . I forgot to tell ya. When we get to my house, there's gonna be a little *surprise*." He emphasized the last word just so.

"What kinda surprise?" Zoey asked. She was hoping for something good, but you could never tell with Logan. Just about everything in Logan's world was about . . . Logan.

"I do *not* like surprises," Nicole said dramatically. "The last time my mom told me I was gonna get a surprise, we took in this foreign exchange student from Guatemala and I swear he stole, like, three of my skirts," she babbled.

The rest of the gang stared at Nicole, not sure

how to respond to that little ramble. Luckily Logan had something else to say.

"Well, this surprise is not bad," he assured them with a nod. As usual, he was the link to something mind-blowing. Just being his friend was going to score the whole gang the most amazing week ever.

Lola looked a little annoyed. What was with all the secrecy? "Well, why can't you just tell us what —"

Just then a dark green van pulled into the PCA drive, honking at the kids waiting on the curb.

"Hey! Over here!" Logan said, waving the van forward like he was an air-traffic controller. The vehicle pulled up and stopped at the curb just beyond the group.

"Mister Reese," one of the men greeted Logan.

Chase smiled. Mister Reese? No wonder Logan thought so highly of himself. Not that Chase was complaining. Already this was looking like one great time away. "Hey, cool, your dad sent a van for us," he said, giving Michael a low five.

Logan smirked. Van, shman. "The van's for our suitcases," he said. He waited exactly five seconds, then turned to the second vehicle pulling into the drive. "That's for us," he finished, looking totally satisfied.

Zoey stared at the vehicle that was rounding the corner. It was by far the biggest, longest, coolest, gleaming white, stretch SUV limo she had ever seen in her life.

"Oh . . ." she said in wonder.

"My . . ." Lola added.

"Whoa!" Dustin was so excited, he started jumping up and down.

"Man, check out this limo!" Michael hooted. Was that a hot tub in the back? Unbelievable!

"I wonder why he sent the little one," Logan said with a smug smile.

"Little one?" Lola echoed with a small nod. She'd always known she was destined to ride in a stretch SUV limo, but she didn't expect it to happen quite so soon!

While the girls squealed with excitement, a couple of men in royal blue polos and shorts got out of the van and started loading the kids' luggage. Suitcases, duffels, and Quinn's lab equipment were all loaded into the back of the van. They had everything ready to go in two minutes flat.

"C'mon, guys!" Logan said, waving his friends over to the limo. He didn't have to ask twice. His friends practically sprinted over and climbed inside, still oohing and aahhing with excitement.

"I'm in a limo!" Dustin shouted.

"Limo! Limo!" Chase chanted happily. Having Logan as a friend had some excellent perks!

"Wooh! Limousine!" Michael chorused as the limo and van convoyed out of PCA and turned onto the Pacific Coast Highway. The gang was finally headed toward Santa Barbara — and the best spring break ever!

"I am in love with this limo!" Nicole exclaimed. If this was the kind of surprise Logan had in mind, it was just fine with her!

"I'm so excited!" Zoey agreed. A whole week with her friends. No classes, no homework, and plenty of fun. What could be better?

Riding in the limo was such a blast, Zoey was shocked when she looked out the window and saw a WELCOME TO SANTA BARBARA sign. She couldn't believe they were already there!

"Whoa! Santa Barbara!" Chase said, looking over her shoulder. The kids all whooped and cheered as the vehicles pulled into a private driveway.

"This is it," Logan announced.

"Ooh, look, they have a gate," Nicole said, impressed.

Of course they did. Anyone who was anyone in Santa Barbara had a gate. "We have arrived," Logan

15

said as the limo pulled to a stop and everyone tum-
bled out.

"Come on," Logan said, waving. He led his friends
past the tennis courts toward the front yard.

"Just a little farther . . ." Logan coaxed. He was
actually feeling really proud to be sharing his house
with his friends. Finally he came to a stop. "And there it
is," he said, turning and gesturing grandly toward his
house.

Everyone stopped and stared at the gorgeous
white mansion sitting on a large, perfectly mani-
cured lawn. Palm trees swayed in the breeze by the
pool and spa. The gardens were immaculate and in full
bloom.

"Is this where you grew up?" Zoey asked, awe-
struck. Logan's house was unbelievably beautiful. More
beautiful than the PCA campus, if that was possible.

"Nah, I grew up in a really *big* house in Beverly
Hills," Logan said, waving the question off. "We spent
summers here."

Zoey was still taking it all in when a man in a tuxedo approached the group and came to a halt right in
front of them.

"Mister Logan," he said through his nose in a
strong British accent.

Logan grinned and gave the guy a rap on the shoulder. "Chaunceeeey!" he greeted, as if they were old friends. "'Sup, buddy?"

Chauncey stood in front of them, looking as stiff as a statue. He eyed the teenagers like they were some kind of alien race. "Yes. Umm . . . your father has arranged an early dinner for you and your friends in the main dining room," the butler reported in a monotone.

"Cool." Logan nodded. "Chauncey, why don't you show everybody their rooms?" he suggested.

The butler didn't move. "That would excite me," he said flatly.

Zoey smirked. Was this guy for real?

Logan acted as if it were perfectly normal to have a butler who was as stiff as cardboard. "Hey, guys — get cleaned up and lookin' nice," he instructed with a knowing smile.

Chase balked. "I have to look nice?" he repeated. Since when were vacations about dressing up?

Michael shook his head. "No one said anything about lookin' nice," he pointed out.

"Why do we have to look nice?" Dustin said, sounding a little disgusted. Would he have to wash his hair?

Logan smiled at his friends. "'Cause after dinner, it's time for the surprise."

Zoey was getting tired of Logan's dangling surprise. "What surprise?!" she asked, not trying to hide her annoyance. But Logan wasn't talking.

After dinner, the gang gathered in a very modern-looking den. Everyone had taken Logan's advice and tried to dress up. And it was undeniable — they looked totally awesome! Zoey wore a black mini-skirt, a glitzy, gold belt, a white cuff bracelet, and she had layered a black tank top over an orange one. Lola looked adorable in a flirty, blue dress, which she paired with a great, retro, butterfly-sleeved, black sweater that had gold accents. Quinn had on tight-fitting jeans and a flowing, peasant-inspired, green shirt. Even the guys dressed up! Logan wore loose-fitting jeans with a black button-down shirt. Michael sported a yellow polo shirt with long, black board-shorts, and Chase chose an orange collared shirt, jeans, and a brown leather cuff bracelet. They were definitely dressed to impress!

Zoey was checking out the scene and thinking she wouldn't mind living in a place like this when she spotted Chauncey standing at the top of a short flight of stairs. A second later he rang a little bell. The kids stopped talking and looked up at him expectantly.

"Adolescents. Your attention, please," he practically shouted. "I give you . . . Logan's father, Mister Malcolm Reese," he finished.

A middle-aged guy in a striped button-down and khakis strolled confidently down the stairs, followed by a very hip-looking woman carrying a clipboard.

Logan burst into spontaneous applause. "Yeah! Dad!" he called, as if his father were a rock star. "All right!"

Zoey shot Logan a look. She was sure his dad was totally cool and everything, but why was Logan acting all star-struck?

"Welcome to my home," Mr. Reese said to the kids warmly. He gestured to the woman behind him as they made their way over to a vintage modern sofa. "This is my assistant, Kira."

"Hey, Kira."

"Hi, Kira."

"'Sup, Kira," the kids greeted.

"Sit down," Chauncey ordered as he followed his employer down the stairs.

Everyone quickly found a seat. You didn't mess with Chauncey. And besides, they were all dying to know what the big surprise was.

Mr. Reese turned to face the kids, who had settled themselves on the sofa and chairs on the other side of the room. "Now, I'm sure you're wondering why you're all here," he said with a knowing smile. It reminded Zoey a little of Logan, actually.

Chase looked a little confused. This was spring break, wasn't it? "Aren't we here to . . . have fun?" he asked with a shrug.

"Well, yes," Mr. Reese agreed. "But there's much more," he said.

Zoey was beginning to see where Logan got his confidence. She gave Nicole a "what's up?" look.

"More?" Nicole echoed.

"Much more," Mr. Reese confirmed, clasping his hands together. "You see, I'm producing a new reality show called *Gender Defenders.* It's a competition to see which sex is better, males . . ."

"Or females," Kira finished.

"*Pfft,*" Logan said from his spot on the sofa. "Like we don't already know," he said cockily.

Lola reached out and squeezed Logan's kneecap until he was begging for mercy — leaving no question about the superior gender.

"And how do we fit into this?" Zoey asked,

getting right to the point. It sounded good so far, but she wanted to know more.

"Good question," Mr. Reese replied. "Well, before you make a TV show, you have to test it. And that's what you guys are going to do." He pointed at the kids with both hands, his smile widening. "We're going to divide you up into two teams: the guys versus the girls. And over the next few days, you'll be pitted against one another in a series of competitions that's gonna test you on three levels: mental, physical, and creative." He ticked off the three categories on his fingers.

Everyone started talking at once. It was clear that in spite of being split into teams, they were in agreement about one thing — this was going to be awesome!

"Wait a minute," Mr. Reese interrupted the kids. "I haven't told you the best part." He paused for effect, then went on. "The team that wins is coming back to Hollywood with me to compete on the very first episode of *Gender Defenders*," he promised.

Now everyone was really talking.

"Wait," Lola squealed. "You're gonna put us on TV?"

Logan rolled his eyes. "No," he said sarcastically.

"He's gonna put *us* on TV." He jerked his thumbs toward himself and the guys.

Lola made a face. "No, he's gonna put *us* on TV," she mimicked. As if.

A second later the two teams were arguing vehemently about who was going to win the competition. It was so loud that Zoey could barely hear her own argument!

"Whoa, whoa, whoa!" Mr. Reese nodded with satisfaction. "This is good. Save it for the competition," he advised.

Next to him, Kira nodded in agreement.

"Now, to say thanks in advance for helping me test my new show, I'd like to give you all a small gift," Mr. Reese said. "Chauncey?"

Zoey watched as the butler carried a small aluminum suitcase over to the coffee table and set it down. He unlatched it and lifted the lid to reveal eight small devices the size of cell phones, each one a different color.

"Whoa, TekMates?" Dustin squealed, leaping to his feet.

All at once the kids jumped up, each taking a gadget from the case. Zoey couldn't believe it. They had a chance to be on TV *and* got TekMates? And they'd only been there for a few hours!

Nicole cradled her bright yellow TekMate lovingly, then realized she had no idea what she was holding. "What are TekMates?" she asked.

"What *aren't* TekMates?" Kira corrected.

"They're a cell phone, address book, MP3 player. . . ." Mr. Reese rattled off.

"They do e-mails, text messaging, Web access. . . ." Kira added.

"And we really get to keep 'em?" Zoey was still in shock, staring at the pink device in her hands.

"Oh, yeah," Mr. Reese confirmed. "And during the competitions, you're free to use them to communicate with your other teammates. Oh, and I forgot. Each side is going to need to select a team captain."

"Zoey?" Nicole suggested questioningly.

"Sure," Zoey agreed with a shrug.

"And I'll be the guys' team captain," Logan announced with a smug smile.

"Well, I think that Chase should be team captain," Michael said.

"Okay, then we'll put it to a vote," Logan said grudgingly. "All those in favor of me for —"

"Chase," Michael and Dustin said at once, cutting Logan off.

"Jerks," Logan huffed, pushing buttons on his

TekMate. They were obviously stupid if they thought Chase's leadership skills could hold a candle to his. But if they wanted to learn the hard way . . .

"Okay. Team captains," Kira said, handing over the rule books. "These are the rules of the competition. You two should meet in the courtyard at ten P.M. to go over them."

"Cool," Zoey said with a smile.

"Thanks," Chase said, taking the book as the rest of the kids filed out of the living room, talking excitedly about the competition.

Chase was following everyone out when Michael grabbed his arm and dragged him back over by the sofas.

"What?" Chase asked, feeling a little too man-handled.

Michael eyed him knowingly. "You and Zoey . . . alone in the courtyard . . . underneath the moonlight?" he said dreamily.

"So?" Chase asked, not sure what his roommate was getting at. He sure hoped it wasn't that Zoey love thing again. Why couldn't Michael just leave him alone!

Michael stared at Chase. How dense was he? "So, it's the perfect time for you to tell Zoey you love her."

Chase stared at Michael. How dense was he? "Man,

when are you gonna stop with that? Is there an OFF button on you anywhere?" He poked at Michael, searching
for the magical spot that would turn off the Zoey talk.

Michael held his hands up to defend himself. "Stop."
He laughed. "Stop. Dude, stop! I'm ticklish."

Chase stopped poking and got serious. "Look, I
told you, my friendship with Zoey is too important. I'm
not gonna risk messin' it up by telling her how I feel."
Chase wasn't sure why his roommate and best friend
was so desperate for him to commit romantic suicide.

"That's insane, man. Listen, I'm tellin' you, all ya
gotta do is just go to Zoey —"

Chase was left with no choice but to go back to
his tickle torture. Poke, poke, poke . . .

"Quit it!" Michael objected with a laugh. "Stop!"

"You like that? You like it? You like it? I hope you
like it. Is this a good experience?" Chase taunted as
Michael collapsed onto the couch in a fit of laughter.

Chase grinned. It was tough torturing a good friend,
but sometimes a person had no choice but to resort to
drastic measures.

CHAPTER 3

Under the Moonlight

Chase waited in the courtyard, tossing a bottle of water into the air and catching it on the back of his hand to pass the time. Where was Zoey?

Suddenly someone cleared his throat. Chauncey.

"May I get you anything, Mister Chase?" he offered.

Chase felt a little stupid. He wasn't used to having people offer to get him stuff. And what was with the Mister? "No, no thank you," he babbled. "I'm just waiting for Zoey."

"Very good, sir," Chauncey said. He turned to walk off, his coattails flapping behind him.

Chase cleared his throat. "Very good, sir," he echoed in a fake British accent. "Very good . . . Mister Chase." He adjusted his button-down shirt and lingered over the words as if he were an actor in a play. "Mister Chase," he repeated again. It had a nice ring.

Suddenly Chauncey reappeared from behind the corner. "Pardon?" he asked rigidly.

Chase flushed. "Oh . . . I was just trying out a British accent, y'know. . . ." he stammered, feeling like an idiot. Just then his TekMate went off. Saved by the beep. "Oooh. I'm beeping. It's my new TekMate," he said, holding the high-tech, blue device up for Chauncey to see. "It's a text message from my friend Michael. He's upstairs," Chase babbled.

Chauncey stared at Chase, expressionless. "That's so interesting," he droned. "I shall go write about it in my blog." He wrinkled his nose as he turned on his heels and disappeared once again.

Chase watched him go. Chauncey was one weird dude. His TekMate beeped again, and he looked down at the tiny screen in his hand. "Look up," he read aloud.

Chase looked directly up to the sky.

"Over here!" came a hoarse whisper.

Chase redirected his gaze to see Michael standing on an upper patio, the full moon shining bright just behind him.

"What?" Chase asked, exasperated. Couldn't a guy

wait in a courtyard without being harassed? Michael was a great friend, but he was driving Chase more than a little nuts.

Michael quickly typed a message on his TekMate. "Tell . . . Zoey . . . you . . . love . . . her," it said. Michael hit SEND.

The gadget in Chase's hand beeped, and Chase read the message. Ugh! Michael was like a broken record. "For the billionth —" Chase whispered hoarsely. Then he stopped himself and looked around nervously. Whew. The coast was clear. But he'd better type his response, just to be safe. "For the billionth time, NO. If I tell Zoey I love her, it could wreck our friendship." Chase hit SEND just as Zoey appeared.

"Hi," she said warmly.

"Oh, Zoey!" Chase started. "Hey." He waved at her a little lamely. Then he smiled. Zoey looked great, as usual. She wore a black tank dress with an orange top underneath, and her blond hair was down around her shoulders.

"So, you wanna go over these rules?" she asked, holding up the book Kira had given her that evening.

Chase felt like a guilty criminal. "Oh, sure," he agreed, trying to ignore his sweaty palms. That was close!

Chase watched Zoey head over to a chair and sit down. As soon as her back was to him, Chase waved Michael away. The last thing he needed was an eavesdropper. Thankfully Michael wasn't the nosy type, and he disappeared just as Chase sat down across from Zoey. Flipping through the rule book, Zoey flashed Chase a smile.

Chase opened his own rule book and groaned inwardly. The next hour was going to be total and complete torture if Michael didn't chill and leave him alone with Zoey.

In the Reese kitchen, Quinn was getting to work on a complex experiment. Different colored liquids bubbled away in beakers of all shapes and sizes. Quinn, who looked funky as usual with her hair in a high ponytail, braided and adorned with ribbons and purple feathers, smelled a couple and tapped a couple more, nodding. She typed a few notes about the formula into her computer. This was going to be good, she could feel it.

"Hey, Quinn," Nicole's friendly voice greeted. "Whatcha makin'?" She peered at the bubbling liquids curiously, careful not to get any on her sequined, lilac tank top. Quinn's experiments used to totally freak her out, but she'd gotten kind of used to them.

"A new energy drink," Quinn replied proudly, looking up from her computer screen. She eyed the hot plates, vials, and fruits on the counter. She loved inventing more than anything.

Nicole wrinkled her nose. "But they already have, like, a million energy drinks," she pointed out. The grocery and sporting goods store aisles were full of them.

"Yes, and they're all full of chemicals and bad things," Quinn replied, sounding a little disgusted. "Which is why I created an all-natural energy drink made of plant extracts, fruit emulsions, and other natural things I've squeezed." She reached down and picked up a blue plastic bottle complete with a lightning-bolt label. "I call it 'Frazz'!" she finished excitedly.

"Frazz?" Nicole echoed, trying out the name. It wasn't terrible. . . .

"Uh-huh," Quinn said with another nod. "Frazz will be one hundred percent healthy and it'll give you seventeen times more energy than any other drink on the market," she vowed.

"So it's ready?" Nicole eyed the blue bottle. To her surprise, she was actually considering trying the drink.

Quinn shook her head, making the feathers on her hair ties swing. "Not yet. It's too powerful. So now I have to figure out a way to make it weaker but still maintain the yummy flavor." She eyed the bottle warily.

"You'll figure it out," Nicole assured her. Quinn was not one to give up on a science experiment. "Hey, I'm gonna go get in the hot tub. Wanna come?"

Quinn nodded. She'd been juicing and squeezing and stirring for hours. A hot tub sounded great. "Sure."

On their way out of the kitchen they spotted a small blond kid coming in.

"Oh, hey, Dustin," Quinn greeted.

"You wanna come hot tub with us?" Nicole offered. Zoey's little brother was always fun to have around.

"Nah, I'm too tired," Dustin said, sounding unusually pooped. "I think I'm just gonna get some juice and go to bed."

"Okay, 'night," Nicole said.

Quinn patted him on the shoulder. *"Ciao."* The girls headed out of the kitchen.

Dustin was on his way to the fridge when he spotted all the hot plates and beakers on the counters. There was experiment stuff everywhere — Quinn had practically taken over the whole room!

"Cool," Dustin murmured as he eyed the bubbling concoctions. Then he spotted the Frazz bottle.

"Frazz," Dustin read aloud, picking it up. He

smelled it, then shrugged. Smelled like juice. *What the heck,* he thought as he took a sip. "Ooooh, that's good stuff," he said aloud. He tipped the bottle again for another gulp. And another. And another. Finally he stopped. "Ahhhhhh." It was thirst-quenching, too.

Dustin's gaze turned to all the stuff in the beakers. What was in there, anyway? Then he noticed that he felt different. His eyes popped open wide, and his body was kinda . . . bouncy. A minute ago he'd felt totally wiped. now he felt . . . energized! Could it be the Frazz?

Dustin wasn't sure, but he knew the stuff tasted great. He lifted the bottle to his lips one last time and polished it off. Awesome!

Setting the empty Frazz bottle on the counter, Dustin bounced out of the kitchen. He had to find something to do — something that would use up some of this energy! Outside he spotted a room with a glass door, and something very interesting on the other side. A stair machine, like the kind they have at the gym.

"Stairs!" Dustin cried, rushing forward.

Two minutes later, Dustin was working out on a stair machine, his skinny little legs pumping up and down like crazy.

"Yeah!" he shouted. "I love this! It's like climbin' stairs, but it never stops!"

Dustin glanced down at the machine's readout. He had already climbed 327 stairs and it felt like nothing.

"Yeah! Stairs rock!" He laughed a little maniacally as he gripped the handlebars tightly and kept climbing. He could do this all night!

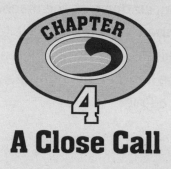

A Close Call

The next morning, Chase woke up early and couldn't get back to sleep. He'd had a blast with Zoey the night before, reading through the rule book and laughing in the moonlight. He really didn't care who won the competition, as long as he and Zoey were friends when it was all over.

Heading down to the den, Chase turned on the TV and settled in to watch some cartoons. A weird-looking alien earthworm was wiggling around on screen.

"What's the big deal about Papluvian Lemonade?" the worm asked.

"Papluvian Lemonade is rumored to be the most delicious beverage in the entire galaxy," a blue tiger replied in a weird alien voice. It reminded Chase of Michael's alien voice, actually.

"I've got the Papluvian Lemonade," a cow bragged. "Beam me up, baby!"

Chase took a swig of orange juice and chuckled at the stupidity of the show. Who wrote this stuff?

"Whassup?!" a loud voice called from the balcony above.

Chase started and shot Michael a look. Did he have to talk so loud? "Hello," he replied, rolling his eyes.

"Man, you woke up early," Michael said, stretching his arms as he trotted down the stairs. He plopped down on the sofa next to Chase. "So . . . how was last night?" he asked, giving him a knowing nudge on the shoulder.

"Whaddaya mean?" Chase asked, shooting his friend a sideways look.

Michael could tell he was going to have to spell it out. "Did you tell Zoey you love her?" he asked bluntly.

"No!" Chase replied hotly, sitting up and turning to face his friend. Zoey could be right around the corner! "I've told you a thousand times, I'm not telling her," he said quietly. "Didn't you read my text message?"

Michael looked confused. "What text message?" he asked.

Uh, hello! "On your TekMate," Chase said. "The one I sent you after you messaged me."

Michael shook his head. "You didn't message me back." Was Chase losing his mind?

"Yeah I did." Chase reached over, grabbed his TekMate, and punched a few buttons. His message appeared on the screen. "Look, man, I wrote, 'For the billionth time, NO. If I tell Zoey I love her, it could wreck our friendship.'"

Michael gave Chase a "you are delusional" look. "Uh, I didn't get that message," he insisted.

"Well, I sent it," Chase repeated.

"Lemme see." Michael leaned over and took the TekMate from Chase. He scrolled through the SENT folder. Uh-oh. Chase sent it all right, but not to him.

"Uh, you didn't send that message to me," he said haltingly.

"I didn't?" Chase asked, confused.

Michael gulped and shook his head. "No."

"Then who'd I send it to?" Chase wanted to know.

Michael winced. He didn't exactly want to tell him, but there was no way out of it. "Zoey," he said in a small voice.

"Zoey?" Chase repeated. Then the name sank in. "Zoey?!?!?!?!" He grabbed the TekMate to see if it was true. His screen confirmed it. His worst nightmare was a reality.

"Oh no!" Chase screamed. "Oh no, oh no, oh no! Michael!"

Michael grabbed a pillow and shoved it in Chase's face to try and quiet him down. Did he want the whole house to hear?

After a lot of screaming, Chase finally pulled it together — sort of. He paced back and forth, trying to figure out what to do.

"This is bad. This is so, so bad," he said miserably.

Michael tried to look on the bright side. "But, you don't know it's bad," he offered.

Chase stared at him in disbelief. What planet was he on? "You don't think it's bad if Zoey finds out I love her from a text message?" he practically shouted.

The dude had a point. "All right, look . . ." Michael was thinking fast. "She didn't have the TekMate with her last night when you guys talked, right?"

"That was last night!" Chase said with a groan. "I'm sure she read it when she woke up this morning!" Why was Michael being so calm? His friendship with Zoey was over!

"Maybe not," Michael said. It was possible, right? "Gimme your TekMate."

Chase handed his TekMate over and Michael pressed a few buttons. A second later the TekMate beeped. "Ha!" Michael said, feeling totally triumphant. "See? Message unread," he reported. "She hasn't seen it yet."

"You're sure?!" Chase asked. It would be a miracle.

Michael pointed to the TekMate screen. It was right there in black and white. Or blue and black and red and white. "Yes!" he promised.

"Okay! Good." Chase was feeling like he might have a way out of this disaster. "I just have to make sure she never sees it," he said, already forming a plan.

"All you gotta do is sneak her TekMate away from her and delete it." Michael made it sound like a piece of cake.

Just then Chauncey strolled by and paused at the bottom of the stairs. "Gentlemen, if you're hungry —" he began.

"Where's Zoey?" Chase shouted at the butler, unable to stay calm.

"Having breakfast," Chauncey enunciated.

"Oh no!" Chase said, leaping over the sofa and bounding up the stairs. He had to get to her TekMate before she did!

Stair Maniac

Zoey, dressed in a black T-shirt, a blue jean skirt embellished with rhinestones, pink dangly earrings, and, of course, her signature key necklace, sat at the counter in the kitchen with Lola, eating breakfast. The food was as incredible as the house — waffles, yogurt, fruit, fresh-squeezed juice. Yum!

"Can you imagine growing up in a house like this?" Lola asked, looking great in a coral tank top, beaded necklace, and black capris.

"I know, it's insane," Zoey agreed. Her house was nothing like this. It was, you know, regular. "Hey, will you pass me those blueberries?" she asked. Blueberries were right under grapes on her favorite fruit list. You could eat them, you could pummel someone with them. . . . The possibilities were endless.

Suddenly Chase's head popped in from around the

corner. He spotted Zoey at the counter, and more important, her TekMate in a little holder on her hip. Crouching
down, Chase stealthily made his way toward Zoey.

"I wonder why they call 'em blueberries," Lola
said thoughtfully, taking a bite of fruit.

"Whaddaya mean?" Zoey asked.

Lola shrugged. "They're purple, not blue," she
pointed out.

Zoey leaned forward and peered into the blueberries on top of her cereal. "Yeah, that's true. Hmmm . . .
y'know, I don't think there even are any blue foods,"
she added thoughtfully.

"There must be some blue food," Lola replied.

"Try to think of one," Zoey challenged, cutting
into her waffles. They looked delicious.

"Okay, ummm . . . let's see. . . ."

Chase barely heard what the girls were saying as
he carefully scooted along under the overhang of the
counter. Finally he was right next to Zoey . . . and her
TekMate. Very slowly he reached a hand up to pull the
pink device out of its holster.

Then, out of the blue, a screechy voice echoed in
the room. "Who touched my Frazz?" it bellowed.

Zoey blinked at Quinn, who was standing on the

other side of the counter, holding up an empty plastic bottle with the word FRAZZ on the front. She had no idea what Frazz was, but Quinn was obviously furious.

"What?" Zoey asked, sliding out of her chair. Chase futilely reached out an arm toward Zoey's TekMate as she walked to the other side of the counter, with Lola right beside her. Opportunity missed!

"What's the matter?" Lola asked.

"My Frazz is gone!" Quinn wailed.

"What is Frazz?" Zoey asked. She didn't get why it was such a big deal.

"The energy drink I'm creating!" Quinn was totally exasperated. Someone had stolen the precious results of her partially created experiment. "This bottle was full of it last night," she explained.

Just then Logan and Michael came into the kitchen.

"Hey, you guys seen Dustin?" Logan asked. Zoey could tell he was a little worried, which was unusual for Logan since he was usually only concerned about himself. . . .

"He's probably asleep in his bed," Zoey said reasonably. Dustin could sleep forever.

"Unh-uh." Michael shook his head.

"We just checked his room," Logan explained.

"His bed hasn't been slept in," Michael added.

Suddenly Quinn looked a little freaked. "What if he drank my Frazz?" she whispered worriedly.

Zoey felt a wave of panic. She still didn't get what Frazz was, but if Quinn was worried . . . and Dustin hadn't slept all night . . .

"Dustin!" Zoey yelled, rushing out of the kitchen. Quinn, Lola, and Logan were right behind her, calling him, too. The foursome split up and started a search party.

Michael hung back in the kitchen. He was starving, and breakfast smelled great. Heading over to the counter, he rubbed his hands together in culinary expectation. "Jackpot," he whispered. There was plenty of food, and no one to have to share it with.

Michael was just reaching for a piece of fruit when something grabbed his ankle.

"Ahhhhh!" he shrieked. He looked down and saw Chase huddled under the counter. "What are you doin'?!" he asked accusingly.

Chase leaped to his feet. "This close," he said, showing a nanospace between his fingers. "I was this close to getting Zoey's TekMate!"

Michael felt for his friend, he really did. But his stomach was growling. "Well, what happened?" he asked.

Chase groaned. "I got Frazzed."

* * *

Meanwhile, the rest of the gang was still searching for Dustin. They checked the bedrooms, the den, the halls. . . . Finally Zoey and Quinn headed out to the gym. Pushing open a sliding glass door, they spotted Dustin on a stair climber. He was laughing like a maniac.

"Oh, hi, Zoey, hi, Quinn, what are you guys doin'? I'm just here on the stair machine, climbin' and climbin'," he babbled. "I really feel like I'm getting good exercise — have you guys had breakfast yet? What'd ya have? I'm not really hungry. This is really fun!" He cackled like a hyena.

Zoey gave Quinn a hard look. Clearly her brother was not normal. Quinn had some explaining to do.

"He drank my Frazz," Quinn said sheepishly.

"How long have you been climbing like that?" Zoey asked, not sure she wanted to know the answer.

"Since last night. Look, I've already climbed . . . over twenty-two thousand stairs!!" he said excitedly.

Twenty-two thousand? Zoey turned back to Quinn. "What's in your Frazz?" she asked accusingly.

"Calm down, it's all-natural," Quinn assured her.

Zoey pointed to Dustin. "That's not natural!" she shouted.

Quinn felt terrible. She never thought anyone would

43

try out her drink without asking about it. And he drank the entire bottle! "The effects should wear off in a few hours . . . or weeks," she said in a small voice.

"Weeks?" Zoey repeated.

Quinn held her hands up in defense. "I'm just a person!" she exclaimed. She felt terrible, but everyone knew that humans were fallible — they made mistakes!

CHAPTER 6

Game On

Suddenly Logan appeared from around the corner. He was out of breath. "C'mon, you guys! The first event's about to start!" he shouted.

"All right!" Dustin yelled. He leaped off the stair machine with as much gusto as he had when he was climbing it. "*Gender Defenders*!" he screamed, jumping down the couple of stairs that led to the outdoor patio. Only he jumped so hard, he fell when he landed. Luckily he barely seemed to notice. Scrambling to his feet, he ran off after Logan, cackling and waving his skinny arms like a cheerleader.

Zoey turned to glare at Quinn. Her brother was totally hyped, and it was more than a little freaky. But Zoey knew there was nothing Quinn could do. And besides, it wasn't really her fault. She'd invented the crazy drink, sure. But it wasn't as if she'd told Dustin to gulp it down. She'd been as surprised as anyone to find the empty bottle this morning.

Quinn winced as she followed Dustin's cackles to the starting point of the competition. Her drink was even more powerful than she'd thought! That was exciting — and more than a little nerve-racking. If only she hadn't left the bottle on the counter . . .

Panting, the girls arrived at the back lawn. The rest of the gang were already there, lined up on the sprawling grass in front of a podium that had been set up on the corner of the patio.

Behind the podium, Kira stood next to Logan's dad. She was holding a thick binder and was smiling warmly at the kids. Off to the side were three hip-looking people Zoey had never seen before.

Zoey squeezed Lola's arm while she waited for Mr. Reese to tell them about the first competition. This was so exciting! And she obviously wasn't the only one who thought so. At the other end of the lineup, the fully Frazzed Dustin could not hold still. He was bopping up and down like a jumping bean.

Mr. Reese stepped up to the podium and leaned into the mic. "Okay. As you know, *Gender Defenders* will be a series of competitions. Now, when we make the actual TV show, we'll have cameras to record everything, but since this is only a test run, it's just gonna be you guys, me, my assistant, Kira . . . and our three judges."

Malcolm waved an arm toward the three cool-looking twenty-somethings on the steps. Of course — they were the judges. They waved at the contestants, and Zoey and her friends gave them a cheer.

Michael clapped along with his friends but wasn't really paying much attention. He was focused on something else — the TekMate sitting in its little holder on Zoey's hip. This was Chase's chance! He gave Chase a quick elbow to get his attention. "Dude," Michael whispered, motioning toward Zoey. "Zoey's wearin' her TekMate."

"I know," Chase whispered back. As if he wouldn't know exactly where Zoey's TekMate and the unread accidental message of love was at every single second! Behind the podium Mr. Reese was going on and on about the competition. Chase barely cared. Did he want to be on TV? Sure. But he cared a lot more about his friendship with Zoey. In fact, it was the most important thing to him. Which was why he was about to swipe her TekMate. . . .

Both boys kept their heads facing front and smiles

on their faces, like the only thing on their minds was *Gender Defenders*. Not.

"She read your message?" Michael whispered quietly.

Chase felt a moment of panic. He hadn't checked since he almost got ahold of Zoey's TekMate in the kitchen.

Chase unsnapped his TekMate from his belt, flipped it open, and pressed a few buttons. "Nope. Still says 'Message Unread.'"

Michael nodded secretively. "So, uh, what are you gonna do?" he asked.

"I'm gonna wait till she's not looking, sneak her TekMate off her hip, delete the message, then put it back," Chase said, giving a little nod. Simple, right? So why was his heart thudding in his chest?

At the podium Mr. Reese paused, letting Kira take the mic. "Your first competition will be mental," she announced.

"A scavenger hunt," Mr. Reese added.

Dustin bounced on the balls of his feet. "What's a scavenger hunt?" he demanded, looking at the adults surrounding him. "What is it?" he asked again, turning to his teammates and bouncing like he was on a pogo stick. "Someone tell me what a scavenger hunt is! C'mon!" he shouted, desperately twisting from one group to the other. "C'mon, c'mon, c'mon." His floppy blond hair made him look like a mop in a windstorm.

Everyone was staring at Dustin like he was a nut-case. Everyone except Zoey. She was giving Quinn the eye. Was her brother *ever* going to be normal again?

Mr. Reese and Kira exchanged glances, then he continued with the instructions. "You see those two safes over there?" He pointed across the large expanse of per-fect lawn. The kids all turned to look at the two brightly colored safes.

As Zoey swiveled, Chase saw his chance. Keeping one eye on Zoey and one ear on the rules, he slowly slid the pink TekMate out of its holder.

"The red safe is for the girls, and the blue safe is for the guys," Mr. Reese explained.

"The only way to open the safes is to have the proper three-digit combination," Kira explained.

The gang turned back to face the podium. Michael took a step forward, planting himself between the unknow-ing Zoey and the scheming Chase. Chase turned away, shielding the TekMate with his body before turning it on.

"Each captain will wait by the safe while their teammates use clues to search for the three digits," Mr. Reese continued.

Chase was barely listening now. He was almost there! The TekMate screen flashed on. He quickly thumbed through the menu and opened messages.

"Once a team finds all three digits, they must deliver the combination to their captain to open their safe." Mr. Reese was still talking, thank goodness. With his heart hammering, Chase located his message and hit DELETE. There! Now all he had to do was slip the TekMate back onto Zoey's hip. . . .

"And the winner of this event will be whichever team captain opens his or her safe and brings me the item inside first." Chase could tell that Mr. Reese was wrapping it up. Luckily Chase was, too. Still holding her TekMate, he took a step closer to Zoey.

"Your first clues are in the envelopes taped to your safes," Kira said with a broad smile. "Ready?" she asked.

Chase inched closer. He reached out his hand just as Mr. Reese held up an air horn.

Zoey smiled. She was definitely ready!

"A-a-and go!" Mr. Reese blasted the horn.

Chase tried to drop the TekMate back into Zoey's holder just as Zoey whirled with her teammates, heading for the safe.

The TekMate slid right past the holder, and Chase nearly fell over. Standing on the lawn still holding the evidence of his crime, Chase groaned. He had successfully deleted the message but had a feeling this little nightmare was far from over.

CHAPTER 7

Safe and Sound

Scrambling to catch up, Chase pocketed Zoey's TekMate. He'd just have to find another chance to get it back to her later. The game was on.

Zoey ran with her shrieking teammates to the far end of the lawn and tore the first clue off of the girls' red safe. She ripped open the envelope and breathlessly handed the clue to Nicole.

"Read it!" the girls clamored.

"Okay!" Nicole said, trying to stay calm. It wasn't easy. She looked down at the small piece of yellow paper in her hand. "It says . . . 'Lola's the secret to finding your first number. Think under her head at night when she slumbers.'"

Behind the girls, the guys were already frantic to catch up. Logan struggled with the envelope. "C'mon, man," Michael said impatiently. "Open it!"

"I'm trying!" Logan shouted back. What did he think he was doing, chilling out? Finally he got it open. "'To find your first digit, here's the way how. Just look underneath the juice of a cow.'"

"The juice of a cow?" Dustin asked, baffled.

"What's cow juice?" Chase asked.

Michael snapped his fingers, trying to come up with the answer.

Meanwhile the girls' team puzzled out their own clue.

"'At night when she slumbers,'" Zoey repeated, holding a hand to her forehead. "'Under her head . . .'"

"Um . . . um . . ." Lola muttered to herself. Sometimes "umming" helped her think.

"Her pillow!" Quinn blurted. It was obvious! All the girls screamed, and Lola, Quinn, and Nicole took off at a run. They were making a beeline to Lola's bed, leaving Zoey to guard the safe and cheer them on.

Beside the blue safe, the guys were still in a huddle.

"Milk!" Logan finally shouted, wagging a finger at his teammates.

"Milk!" Michael repeated. "The refrigerator! C'mon!"

Logan, Dustin, and Michael hauled butt toward the kitchen.

"Michael," Chase shouted after them. "I have a problem!" He pointed at the pocket where he had stashed Zoey's TekMate.

Michael barely turned. "Later!" he shouted back, leaping up the stairs to the house. What could he possibly do now?

Nicole, Quinn, and Lola rushed into Lola's guest room and scrambled onto the huge bed, tossing red, orange, and yellow pillows everywhere. There were so many pillows, it was impossible to tell which one had the clue on it without looking at them all.

Finally they got to the striped pillow at the bottom. Lola turned it over and spotted a red envelope with the number fourteen printed on the outside. "Fourteen!" she squealed.

"Fourteen!" Quinn and Nicole shrieked in unison.

"Okay, okay, okay, the first number is fourteen!" Lola said, calming down a little.

"Good!" Nicole said, taking a deep breath. They had their first number, but they still had two to go. "Now open it and read our next clue!" she directed her teammates.

Quinn clutched the yellow paper tightly and pushed her glasses up on her nose. "'Your second digit is now what you need, so look in a place where you cook with great speed,'" she read clearly.

Lola peered at the clue over Quinn's shoulder. "Okay, okay. Uh, 'cook with great speed . . .'"

Nicole looked up at the ceiling, wondering where the speediest cooks were located. She had it! "France!" she shouted. Weren't there quick cooks in France?

Lola looked at her goofy friend, totally exasperated. "Yes, Nicole, now we all run to France," she said sarcastically. What was the girl thinking?

Nicole shrugged. At least she was offering up answers!

"A microwave!!!" Quinn suddenly shouted.

Of course! All three girls screamed and ran out of the bedroom, tossing pillows as they went.

The guys were already there. Throwing open the giant refrigerator, Dustin scanned the shelves for cow juice. "Where's the milk?" he yelled.

"Here!" Logan grabbed a carton and tipped it over. A blue envelope with a number on it was taped to the bottom. "Twenty-seven!" he exclaimed. One down, two to go. They'd be winning this competition pronto.

"Okay, the first number's twenty-seven!" Michael announced, pulling the envelope off the carton while Logan shut the fridge.

"Read the next clue!" Dustin shouted. He was still so hopped up on Frazz that he couldn't stand still, even for a second. The older boys were almost as hopped up from the adrenaline of the game.

"'To learn your next number, you don't need a teacher. You just need to visit an adorable creature,'" Logan read.

"Adorable creature?" Dustin was baffled.

But the two words made Michael think of something . . . or someone. "Lisa Lillien!" he said, snapping his fingers.

"Who's Lisa Lillien?" Logan asked, shooting Michael a look. The dude was starting to look all dreamy.

"This adorable girl who lived down the street from me, man." Michael stood up straight, reminiscing about this incredibly cute neighbor. "She had these teeth . . ."

"Focus, dude!" Logan shouted, whacking Michael's shoulder with the back of his hand. They didn't have time for this. He had to reel Michael in, and fast.

"Hey, didn't you say your dad has a pet rabbit?" Dustin asked, bouncing up and down and peering at Logan.

"Yeah?" What was the kid getting at?

"Adorable creature!" Michael said, wide-eyed, waiting for Logan to get it.

Logan got it. "Yes. C'mon!" Logan sprinted out of the kitchen with Michael and Dustin on his heels.

As the guys ran out one door, Nicole, Quinn, and Lola ran in another.

"Okay. Where's the microwave?" Lola asked.

"There!" Quinn pointed.

Nicole pressed a button and pulled the handle on the sleek black appliance. They were right again. The clue was on the inside of the door. "Seven!" Nicole yelled before pulling off the clue.

"C'mon, only one number to go!" Lola said encouragingly. They were doing great. Her television debut was so close, she could almost taste it.

"Open it!" Quinn was feeling anxious.

"Okay, ummm . . . 'For your final digit, just look to the north, on the special red seat that flies back and forth,'" Nicole read.

The three girls looked at one another. They looked around the kitchen, then back at one another. Nobody said anything. Nobody had a clue.

"'Flies back and forth,'" Nicole read again. She had absolutely no idea. "What?" she asked nobody in particular.

"What does that mean?" Lola cried, waving her arm in frustration. The rhyme made no sense!

Outside, Michael, Dustin, and Logan rounded the east gardens and kept running until they got to the bunny hutch. A black-and-white lop-eared rabbit was happily munching his morning meal inside the cage. And more important, hanging next to the bunny on a string was the guys' next and final clue.

"Hey, Cookie!" Logan greeted as he opened the cage and retrieved the clue. There was no time to pat his dad's pet now.

"Twelve!" the guys read the number on the envelope. They were two-thirds of the way there.

"Twelve! Twelve!" Dustin and Michael chanted.

"One more number to go!" Michael said, waiting for Logan to read the clue. Beside him, Dustin bounced and waved his arms.

"Okay." Logan read, "'For your final digit, just look to the north, on the special blue seat that flies back and forth.'"

The three guys looked at one another. They looked around at the yard, then back at one another. They had no clue.

"What does that mean?" Michael held his hands out in frustration.

Logan was practically pulling out his curly brown hair. "Which way's north?" he gasped.

Nobody answered. The only sound the boys heard was Cookie, chewing away.

In the kitchen, the three girls were still racking their brains.

"What kinda seat goes back and forth?" Lola asked, pacing. She could feel her chances of being on TV slipping away. She had to come up with the answer.

Nicole was really starting to panic. They had to win this round of the competition! "Other than a swing?" she added.

"A swing!" Quinn shouted. It was so obvious that they'd totally missed it.

"Let's go!" Lola shouted. A second later all three of them were screaming and running down the hall to find a swing.

Back at the hutch, Cookie was still eating and the guys were still thinking.

"'A blue seat that goes back and forth . . .'" Logan was hoping that if he just repeated the clue enough times, the answer would come to them. And it did.

"Do you have a swing set?" Dustin suddenly shouted.

"Swing set!" Logan repeated. That was it. "Yes!" he yelled, pumping his fist in the air.

"C'mon!" Michael grabbed Logan by the arm. There would be time to celebrate later. Right now they had to get to that swing set!

With Dustin in the lead, the guys tore around the corner of the house toward the swings. Quickly the over-energized kid flipped the blue seat over and grabbed the clue.

"Thirty-six!" he yelled.

"Thirty-six," the guys echoed.

"So our combination is twenty-seven/twelve/thirty-six!" Michael announced. They had everything they needed. Now they just had to get it back to Chase before the girls did.

The minute Michael remembered the competition, the three squealing girls came sprinting across the lawn. They had solved their final clue as well and were scrambling to get the number.

Panting, Lola, Quinn, and Nicole ripped their final red envelope off the swing and read the number.

"Twenty-one!" Lola shouted.

"Our combination's fourteen/seven/twenty-one!" Quinn put it all together for them.

Logan refused to be distracted by the screaming girls. "Michael," he yelled, "you're the fastest! Take these numbers to Chase so he can open the safe!"

Michael shook his head and refused the clues. "I'm not the fastest when he's all full of Frazz!" he said, pointing at Dustin. The younger kid was vibrating so fast, it was hard to focus on him.

"Yeah! Yeah!" Dustin agreed. He didn't want to stop moving fast, ever. "Gimme those!" He grabbed the numbers and took off like a shot — yelling and laughing all the way.

"Go, kid!" Michael shouted after him.

"C'mon!" Logan motioned to Michael, and the two bigger guys took off after speedy D.

"Which one of us is fastest?" Nicole asked desperately. The guys were obviously getting ahead.

"Not me," Quinn frantically explained. "I have an extra toe on my right foot."

"It doesn't matter!" Lola interrupted. Now was not the time for a weird Quinn fact. "We can't outrun the guys!" They needed another solution.

Quinn gasped. "TekMate!" she cried.

Nicole was confused. "What about it?" TekMates didn't have wheels. Did they?

"We'll text message the combination to Zoey!" Quinn spoke so fast, she was hard to understand.

"Quinn, you're brilliant!" Nicole squealed, jumping up and down. They were going to win!

"Just do it!" Lola reined them in. They had to get the job done, and fast.

"Right!" Quinn flipped open her TekMate and started typing the numbers Nicole held in her hand. "Uh, uh . . . fourteen . . . seven . . . twenty-one . . . and send!"

"Okay, okay, let's go." Lola led the way back to the red safe and their team leader, who should have already received their message — and the winning combination. Thanks to amazing communication technology, she was one step closer to going to Hollywood!

CHAPTER 8

The Right Combination

Zoey stood by her safe and waited nervously, tapping her foot and trying to see around the corner. She knew her team was good, but would they be faster than the guys? Beside her, Chase seemed even more nervous than she was. He kept bouncing on the balls of his feet, waving at her and smiling with only half his face.

Maybe Logan's dad and the judges were making him tense. They were standing nearby, holding their clipboards and talking to one another in low tones, like something was up.

Finally Zoey heard shouting coming from the house. But it wasn't her teammates — it was her brother.

Dustin was barreling toward Chase like a banshee. Behind him, Logan and Michael were breathless just trying to keep up. Running out the sliding glass doors, Dustin leaped over all four steps down to the lawn, hit the ground, and kept going.

"Here comes the kid," Mr. Reese remarked, watching the guys whiz past.

"Twenty-seven/twelve/thirty-six!" Dustin yelled. He shoved the numbers into Chase's hand and Chase began dialing as fast as he could.

"Hurry!" Logan shouted, slapping Chase on the shoulder blade. He was so out of breath, he could barely talk. The Frazzed Dustin was a speedster.

"Turn the dial!" Michael panted, running up behind Logan. "Hurry up, c'mon."

Chase turned the dial carefully. If he went too fast, he'd miss a number and have to start over. "Twenty-seven," he said, stopping on the first digit.

He spun the dial in the other direction. "Twelve," he announced when he'd arrived. He looked over his shoulder for the girls' team. There was no sign of them. Only one more number and open sesame. . . .

"Thirty-six," he called to his teammates. He lifted the handle on the locker, and it slid open, revealing the mystery item inside.

Chase squinted at the contents of the safe, confused.

A second later he pulled a frosty glass of amber liquid from the shelf inside. "Iced tea?" he said, baffled.

"Just —" Michael did not care what it was. He wanted Chase to get with the program and deliver the contents to Mr. Reese — and fast! Hadn't he been listening to the instructions before the race?

Chase got the point. He ran the bewildering beverage over to the television producer and handed it over, waiting to hear that they had won.

As if he had all the time in the world, Mr. Reese raised the drink to his lips, took a sip, and savored it. After he swallowed and looked at the judges for confirmation, he finally spoke. "And the guys win the event!" he announced, beaming. He blew his air horn.

Zoey walked slowly away from her post toward the podium, watching the boys jump on one another and hug like football players in a victory pile-up. She felt totally deflated. Where were her girls? She'd figured the competition would at least be close.

At last Quinn, Lola, and Nicole jogged up to the assembled crowd. For losers, they looked awfully happy.

"Did we win?" Nicole asked. There was genuine excitement in her eyes. Didn't she see the victory party going on next to her?

"How could we win?" Zoey held her hands palm up in frustration. "You didn't bring me the combination!"

The smiles on her friends' faces faded in an instant.

"We text messaged it to you!" Nicole exclaimed, feeling miserable. She really thought they'd won. "You didn't get it?"

Zoey looked down at her belt. "No!" she said. The little strap that held her TekMate in its holster was unsnapped and the holder was empty. Her head jerked up. "Hey, where's my TekMate?"

"You had it when we started!" Nicole said. She remembered seeing it on Zoey's hip during the announcements.

"Here, I'll call your phone number," Quinn said logically. She already had her own TekMate out and was pressing buttons. Leave it to Quinn to come up with a quick fix.

A few feet away, Chase was eyeing the girls nervously. He'd heard their whole conversation — everyone had. And now that Quinn was dialing, there was no way he'd get out of everyone knowing that he had Zoey's —

The girly ring tone emanating from Chase's pocket tragically interrupted his thoughts. The guys' party was over.

One by one, the girls — and everyone else gathered on the lawn — looked over at Chase. Zoey turned to face him, and her expression made Chase wince. She was clearly furious.

Chase tried one of those "I'm just gonna pretend this isn't happening and maybe it will all go away" whistles. As usual, it didn't work.

"Chase?" Zoey looked even more confused than Chase had felt when he found the iced tea in the safe.

There was no getting out of this one. Chase reached into his pocket. "I, um, I found it," he said lamely as he pulled out Zoey's pink TekMate.

"You took Zoey's TekMate?" Lola could not believe what she was seeing. Chase had always seemed like such a good guy — she'd never have pegged him as a cheater.

"Well . . . I . . . I sorta . . ." Chase tried desperately to think of an excuse. He wasn't trying to sabotage the girls. He was trying to unsabotage himself!

"That's cheating!" Nicole said, clearly outraged.

"No," Logan defended his buddy — and more important, his win. "That's smart strategy," he insisted.

"It's cheating," Lola said flatly. There was no denying that Chase had crossed the line.

Quinn was disgusted. "I can't believe you'd want to win this way," she said, shaking her head.

"I don't!" Chase insisted. How could he make them see?

Michael stood behind his friend. He wished there was something he could do, but what? "Chase wouldn't cheat," he said. Everyone there knew it wasn't the dude's style. Didn't they?

"Well, Logan's dad said we could use our TekMates to communicate!" Lola pointed out.

"And Chase took it to sabotage our communications!" Quinn was getting really mad.

"No, I really didn't!" Chase insisted. But if he told them the real reason he'd taken it he would have to come clean about everything. And as dire as things were looking at the moment, he just wasn't ready for that.

"Then why'd you take it?" Lola pressed. She crossed her arms over her chest and waited for an answer. Her expression clearly said, "This had better be good."

Chase looked at the girls' faces. There was a lot of anger there. And Zoey's expression was the worst of all. She just stood there with her hands on her hips, looking kind of . . . disappointed.

"Just tell me why you took it and I'll believe you didn't cheat," she said earnestly.

Chase felt his heart sink. He wanted to tell her

the truth, he really did! Except he couldn't. He couldn't risk losing her friendship.

"Tell me why," Zoey repeated.

Chase shot Michael a desperate look. What was worse, having your best friend think you're a cheat, or losing your best friend because she finds out you love her?

Michael shrugged. What could he say? There was no easy answer.

Lola took Chase's silence as proof of his guilt. "See?" she said hotly. "I told you he cheated!"

The look in Zoey's eyes was too much for Chase to take. "I can't believe you'd do this," she said, shaking her head. Snatching her TekMate out of his hands, she pushed past him and walked into the house with her whole team following her — glaring at Chase as they went.

This was getting worse and worse. Chase watched Zoey head into the house. "Zoey . . ." he called after her. But Zoey didn't even look back.

There was only one thing to do: go after her. Chase took the stairs two at a time. He had to straighten this out ASAP.

Logan shrugged. He had no idea what that was about, but it didn't really matter. "At least we won," he said with a shrug.

Michael and Dustin gave Logan the stink eye. Leave it to Logan to think of himself at a moment like this!

Mr. Reese, Kira, and the judges had watched the whole thing in silence. Finally, after the girls were gone, Kira spoke her mind. "You're not going to disqualify the boys?" she asked her boss.

"Well, I can't disqualify 'em," Mr. Reese said with a shrug not unlike his son's. Kira looked harder at Mr. Reese, waiting for him to explain. "Logan's my son," he added, sheepishly taking a sip of iced tea. Like son, like father.

Disgusted, Kira rolled her eyes and walked away. Mr. Reese barely seemed to notice. He took another sip of his drink.

"Ooh, that's good tea," he said to no one in particular.

CHAPTER 9

Lie, Cheat, and Steal

Zoey stormed back up to the house and around the side porch to the ramp that led to her guest room. Chase was still behind her, calling her name, but Zoey was too mad to even turn around. She needed some time to think and cool off.

"Zoey . . . Zoey . . ." Chase sounded pathetic. What did he want? What could he possibly say to make this mess okay? "Zoey, come on . . ." Chase pleaded.

Finally Zoey turned. She looked hard at Chase. How could she explain how betrayed she was feeling? "You're the last person in the world I thought would cheat," she told him. She trusted Chase. He was the first boy she'd met at PCA, and they'd become fast friends. They shared stuff and helped each other out. He was her go-to guy. The guy she trusted.

"I didn't cheat!" Chase insisted.

"You took my TekMate!" Zoey exclaimed. It was a fact; they had all seen him pull the device out of his pocket.

"I know." Chase shrugged. He looked sheepish, and more than that — ashamed. "I did," he admitted.

"And that made us lose the event," Zoey continued logically.

"I didn't mean for that to happen," Chase explained. That was definitely the truth!

Zoey looked hard at Chase. He seemed like he was being honest, but . . . "All the girls think you did."

"So? Just because they think I'm a liar and a cheater, you have to think it, too?" Chase asked pointedly. Hadn't a year and a half of friendship proven anything to Zoey? Didn't she know him at all?

"Okay, don't try to turn this around on me," Zoey said hotly. She was not on trial here — Chase was. And he was getting really defensive.

"I just can't believe you'd accuse me of —"

"I'm not accusing you of anything!" Zoey exclaimed, cutting Chase off. "I'm saying, 'Tell me the truth!' Tell me why you took my TekMate and I'll believe you!" It was not too much to ask.

Chase pushed his hands into his pockets. He took a deep breath, looked at Zoey, and looked away. "I, uh, I can't," he said.

"Why?" Zoey asked. She didn't understand. What was so hard about a simple explanation? What in the world would Chase want to keep from her? "What are you hiding?"

Chase could not answer the question, so instead he told Zoey the most important other truth he could think of. "Zoey, I didn't cheat." He looked her right in the eye. "You know I'm an honest guy," he added.

Zoey sighed. She *used* to know that. But then again, she used to know a lot of things. "Honest people don't hide things," she said sadly. Then, with one more look, she brushed past him and walked back down the ramp.

Chase stared after her. "And now you're just walking away?" he asked.

"Yep," Zoey answered without turning around.

"So what does this mean?" Chase called after her, afraid of the answer but desperate to know what was going on. "We're not friends anymore?"

Zoey stopped. Slowly she turned back. Her brown eyes bored into Chase. He felt like he'd been punched in the chest. The look was not angry — it was hurt, and worse, disappointed. Chase slumped against the rail. All he had been trying to do was save his friendship with Zoey.

He'd ruined it anyway.

Nerd Makeover

The next day the mood of the *Gender Defenders* was a little different. Everyone except Frazzified Dustin seemed a little down. Zoey and Chase still weren't talking, and the pressure was on for the girls to even the score.

Standing beside the lap pool, Kira and Mr. Reese were calling the shots. "Your next event will be a creative challenge," Mr. Reese enunciated. "Nerd makeovers."

Michael raised his eyebrows and his hand. "What's a nerd makeover?" he asked.

Kira shot him a look. "It's when you give a nerd a makeover," she spelled out.

Michael nodded knowingly, trying to save face. "Ahhh," he said, lowering his hand and feeling like a dork. Now that he had the answer, it did seem kind of obvious.

Logan groaned and swatted his teammate. What was he, six? Duh. He was already making the guys look bad, and they had to look sharp. Today was victory day!

Chauncey stepped forward. As usual, he looked stiff and overdressed in his tuxedo. "Let's meet the nerds," he said slowly in his English accent. He motioned toward the *Gender Defenders'* victims.

"First, from Fresno, California, I'd like you to meet Marty Felzenberg," Mr. Reese spoke as if he were introducing contestants in a pageant.

A guy in his twenties slouched around the pool landscaping and waved goofily.

"Marty just got his master's degree in geology. He's twenty-six years old and has never kissed a girl," Kira said, filling in the details. But Marty's outfit pretty much said it all. He was dressed in a geeky plaid button-down shirt that was buttoned all the way up and pleated khakis that he'd tucked into his socks. His black-framed glasses were thick, and his wavy hair was parted in the middle and plastered down.

"Now, that's a dork," Logan confirmed cockily.

Nicole swatted him. That wasn't nice! And besides, what if they got stuck with that loser?

"Next, from Davenport, Iowa, please say hello to Nelson Parnell," Mr. Reese welcomed the next nerd.

Zoey blinked as a second guy appeared from behind the poolside shrubbery. If anything, the second guy was worse than the first. He was shorter, had slicked-back hair, and wore a light blue windbreaker. If his clothes left any doubt of his doofiness, Kira's details cleared it up.

"Nelson collects antique swords, has an impressive coin collection, and loves vacationing with...his mother," Kira said with a smile.

Nelson shrugged, grinning. He looked almost proud, and Zoey was certain he could talk for hours about every single one of those coins in that collection of his.

"Your mission" — Mr. Reese paused briefly for effect — "is to take these two losers and make them... incredibly cool."

Whoa, Lola thought. *Talk about mission impossible!*

"The guys' team gets Marty. Girls, you get Nelson." Kira directed each geek toward his team.

From behind the group of kids, Chauncey spoke again in his pompous drawl. "All the materials you'll need are to the left of my gesture," he said. He pointed to the left and behind him, and Zoey spotted racks of clothes and tables piled with grooming products, accessories, and more.

"Are both teams ready?" Kira asked.

"Ah, just . . . can I ask one question?" Michael waved his hand in the air.

"No," Mr. Reese replied before blowing his air horn. "The nerd makeover!"

Both teams grabbed their nerds and hustled them toward the waiting materials.

First things first. In a matter of minutes the girls had stripped Nelson down to his boxer shorts and Nicole was hosing him down. The pathetic geek hopped around in the freezing water. He looked so miserable that Nicole almost felt bad. But if there was a price to be paid for terrible fashion sense, this was it. Nobody ever said being cool was easy!

The guys were no less harsh with Marty. Michael did the honors with the hose while Marty spun in frantic circles, complaining about the cold. There was no time for a hot bath — a cold hose was the best they could do.

After their dousings, Nelson and Marty were hastily ushered to a pair of salon chairs and sloppily shampooed before being drenched as a final rinse.

Nelson flapped his hands in front of the cold stream of water like a trained seal. Both geeks struggled to hang on to their glasses.

Clean and dressed in T-shirts and shorts, the nerds were seated once more in the styling chairs. Now it was time for the real work to begin.

"Get rid of his nose hairs!" Nicole squealed in horror at the growth coming out of Nelson's nose. Dispensing with that thatch was essential.

Zoey grabbed a trimmer and went to work, ignoring Nelson's cries of pain.

"Fix his eyebrows!" Dustin barked to the blue team. The woolly caterpillars over Marty's eyes needed serious taming.

Michael began to pluck with impunity while Marty squealed in pain. No pain, no gain. Looking cool took work!

"Mommy!" Nelson called from his chair. His feet vibrated in the air. He was obviously in pain, and Zoey felt for the guy. But the results would be worth it. And the girls needed the win!

When the facial hair was under control, the girls started to tackle the hair on the top of Nelson's head. Lola busted out the blow-dryer and some grooming cream. Nicole wielded a comb. And Nelson was starting to look a lot better. But what in the world was he reading?

Lola peered over his shoulder while she blew-dry his hair. Was that an article about the life cycle of the monarch butterfly? Lola snatched the magazine out of his hands and checked the cover. Sure enough, *Fabulous Butterflies*. Not acceptable, and definitely not cool. Lola disgustedly tossed the magazine aside.

Finally Nelson's face and hair were done — it was time for clothes. Leave it to the geek to grab the only bad shirt on the rack they had to choose from!

Nicole made a face and stared at the shirt as if it were a dead animal.

"Gross," Zoey proclaimed.

Thankfully Nicole grabbed the hideous blue plaid and buried it back on the rack.

Several feet away, the guys struggled to dress Marty. He didn't look too terrible in a sports jacket, T-shirt, and jeans, except for the fact that he kept hitching the jeans up to his armpits. It made him look like Michael's grandpa! Fully annoyed, Michael yanked the pants back down low, settling them on Marty's hips.

Three outfits later, the girls' team settled on a red button-down shirt, striped blazer, jeans, and flip-flops. Nelson was looking good, but something was missing. Nicole slid a pair of cool sunglasses on him, and he looked around as if he were an actor on a movie set. The girls checked out their handiwork and nodded with satisfaction. Nelson was looking totally California cool.

Now that Marty's jeans were looking acceptably hip, the boys got down to accessorizing. The final touch was a pair of rectangular specs with wide temples.

"Looking good!" Lola congratulated as the girls dragged Nelson full tilt toward the judges. The guys and their geek were right behind them.

Just as both teams halted before the judges, Mr. Reese blew the air horn. "Time's up!" he crowed. "Let's see the results."

Ready for judging, the red team stood on one side of Logan's dad and his crew, and the blue team stood on the other. Their transformed nerds were carefully hidden behind them until the moment of unveiling arrived.

Zoey was so nervous and excited, she almost forgot about her fight with Chase.

The guys revealed their geek first.

"Ladies and gentlemen," Michael announced, gesturing with his arm to their coolified nerd, "the newly transformed Marty Felzenberg!"

"All right!" Logan and the other guys cheered. Marty was looking good!

Logan and Chase parted, and Marty stepped forward, looking way cooler than he had before. He now wore a faded peachy-tone T-shirt layered with a dark red button-down shirt (unbuttoned), a brown blazer, and low-slung jeans. His hair was styled but just messy enough. He gave a point-and-shoot gesture to the judges, who clapped politely, nodded approval, and made some quick notes on their clipboards.

Next up was the girls' team. Zoey held her breath. It was too exciting!

"Everyone, I give you the revised Nelson Parnell!" Quinn squealed, pointing toward the guy who was standing behind her teammates. The girls stepped to the side and a very laid-back Nelson came forward. He did a double point-and-shoot and gave a nod to the judges. The thin white stripes in his blazer brought out the super-trendy white belt laced in his low-rise jeans. And his hair was looking hot, kind of spiked up and defined. Even the guys' team looked impressed.

Both guys were extremely improved. Nobody would say they looked like nerds now. Mr. Reese, Kira, and the other judges looked pretty blown away. It was going to be a tough decision.

Nicole, Zoey, Lola, and Quinn talked nervously while the judges conferred. They seemed to have a lot to talk about. But what were they saying?

At last Mr. Reese and Kira turned to face the two

teams. The lead judge handed Mr. Reese a card, which he unfolded and read. "And the winner is . . ."

All eight kids waited. They stood stock-still and said nothing. Nobody breathed.

"The girls!" Mr. Reese finished.

Squeals and cheers erupted from the girls, who came together in a giant hug. They'd won! The match was officially tied!

"Aw, come on, man!" Logan complained loudly. "He vacations with his mother!"

Zoey heaved a huge sigh of relief. Cheating or no cheating, they still had a chance to win. A good chance.

Dustin stared up at Marty and his teammates. They all looked like the world was coming to an end.

"Aw, man, we lost!" Dustin said, dropping his hands to his sides. Then he smiled. "I'm gonna run in circles!" He raced around the group, going faster and faster and laughing like a lunatic.

Michael looked at the spazzy kid like he could not believe what he was seeing. That Frazz stuff was serious.

And the Winner Is . . .

Later that day the *Gender Defender* teams waited anxiously on the lawn to learn what the final event would be. They were beat from the earlier events. Competing against your friends was exhausting! Plus, it was sweltering out.

The only person who didn't look like a melting candle was Dustin. While everyone else tried to ignore the heat, he did jumping jacks.

Mr. Reese and Kira both looked cool as Hollywood cucumbers, as usual. They stood at the podium facing the kids. The judges held their verdict at the side of the stairs.

"Okay!" Mr. Reese looked almost as excited to hear the final results as the kids. "That completes the first two events of the competition. Judges?"

Everyone looked at the judges.

"We have a tie." One of the judges shrugged.

"So how do we break it?" Logan shouted.

Quickly Mr. Reese consulted with his assistant and the big black binder.

Kira leaned in and spoke into the mic. "The tie will be broken with a physical challenge," she said.

"Between the two team captains, Zoey Brooks and Chase Matthews," Mr. Reese added, pointing to each of the former friends in turn.

Zoey took a deep breath and looked over at her ex-friend. This was not going to be fun, or easy.

Chase felt a little sick as he eyed Zoey. A head-to-head physical challenge with Zoey was the last thing he wanted to do at this moment. But they didn't know exactly what they had to do yet. Maybe it wouldn't be so bad. . . .

A few minutes later the teams and their captains had been debriefed. They were all standing around the pool. And the challenge wasn't bad. It was horrible.

"The aqua battle!" Mr. Reese shouted, pumping his fist as he approached the pool. Everyone was already in position.

The team captains faced each other, balanced on underwater pedestals about four feet apart. From the side of the pool, where their teammates stood watching in their bathing suits, it looked like Zoey and Chase were walking on water. In their hands, each captain held what appeared to be an enormous and colorful Q-tip. They were actually five-foot battle batons with padded ends — red for Zoey and blue for Chase. The captains were wearing helmets and tank tops and shorts over their suits — all in team colors, of course.

"When the horn sounds, each team captain will try to knock the other off his or her pedestal and into the water," Kira explained, beaming.

"The first one to be knocked into the water two times loses," Logan's dad added, waving his air horn in the air.

Zoey eyed Chase. She was still really sad and hurt about the cheating, and was looking to take Chase out. Two times would be easy.

"And to make it more interesting, the rest of you will use those turbo soakers to spray your opponent, in order to help your team captain win." Kira pointed at a pair of racks of red and blue turbo soakers.

"Okay, pick up your soakers and take your positions," Mr. Reese directed.

The guys grabbed the blue soakers and stood

behind Chase, carefully aiming the pump-action water guns at Zoey.

The girls got behind Zoey and leveled their red weapons at Chase.

"Are the teammates ready?" Kira asked.

"Yes," the guys all yelled. Logan couldn't wait. Soaking Zoey was going to be a blast, and Chase should be able to take her down easily. She was just a girl, right?

Michael gave a thumbs-up. He was ready and waiting, with soaker in hand.

The girls shouted their agreement from the other side of the pool. As far as Lola was concerned, it was time to make Chase pay for his mistakes.

"Captains! Are you ready?" Mr. Reese asked.

"Yeah." Chase nodded without smiling. He was as ready as he'd ever be.

"Let's go," Zoey said. She had her game face on and was hoping she could back it up with a win.

"Fight!" Mr. Reese shouted, blowing his air horn.

The battle was on! Chase took the first swing, but Zoey ducked. Then she swung, and Chase blocked. Over and over, the ex-friends swung at each other, each trying to knock the other down while the opposing team members blasted them with water.

Lola, Nicole, and Quinn kept up a steady stream on Chase, pausing only to reload by pumping water from the pool into their soakers. Nicole was feeling totally frantic. Zoey had to win!

The guys drenched Zoey in seconds, pummeling her with water. But Zoey ignored it and focused on Chase's baton. She was giving as good as she got, but suddenly Chase faked her out. Swinging his baton up from below, he took her by surprise and sent her backward off the pedestal.

The girls jumped back, staring at Zoey in shock and horror.

The guys cheered and slapped fives with one another.

"Yes!"

"Go, Chase!"

"Guys rule!" they shouted.

Chase barely heard them. He was too busy waiting for Zoey to come up to the surface. When she finally did, Chase winced. She didn't look happy.

"C'mon, Zoey!" the girls cheered.

"You can do it."

"Get back up there," Nicole yelled as Zoey spit water. Zoey scowled. What did she think she was going to do, give up?

Zoey carefully avoided Chase's eyes as she climbed back up onto the pedestal.

"Are you okay?" Chase asked. He looked really sorry.

"I'm fine," Zoey answered flatly. She couldn't help but think how sorry he was going to be when she took him out.

"Round two!" Mr. Reese blew his horn and they were back on.

Zoey and Chase swung and blocked while the turbo soakers rained down on them. After blocking several swings, Zoey saw her chance. She quickly got her baton centered and butted Chase backward off his platform.

Zoey smiled and looked back at her cheering teammates. They were one step closer to winning, and she felt . . . awful. Why did Chase have to steal her TekMate? Why couldn't he just tell her the truth?

"That's what I'm talking about," Quinn said, slapping hands with Nicole and Lola.

Across the pool, Logan looked like he was going to explode. "How could you do that?" he yelled at Chase. The dude was making them look like sissies!

"What was that?" Michael asked. Chase obviously wasn't in top form.

"C'mon, Chase!" Even Dustin sounded disappointed.

"Get back up on that platform," Logan demanded. As if Chase had a choice.

Spluttering and shaking his head, Chase climbed back up. He was beginning not to care who won and who lost. He just wanted this whole thing over.

"All right," Kira announced. "The next one to go in the water loses."

"Round three!" Logan's dad hit the air horn again.

This was it. They were down to the wire. Zoey swung with all of her might, ignoring the soakers. Chase struggled but stayed up. He took a jab at Zoey. She wavered for an instant, then hit him back harder.

Chase came at Zoey with an overhand twist — an unusual move. A second later Zoey's baton fell into the pool.

For a moment both of them stared at the red baton floating in the water. Zoey had been disarmed!

The teams on the sidelines were going nuts.

"Oh no, she lost her thingy!" Lola shrieked. Nicole and Quinn could barely look. This had to be the end.

But Chase just stood there while his teammates freaked out.

"Yessss!" Logan cried, jumping up and down. "You got her. Take her down!"

"Do something," Michael said.

Chase heard his teammates as clear as anything. They wanted him to go in for the kill. To win the match. To take them all to Hollywood. But Chase hesitated. This wasn't how it was supposed to be. Shaking his head, he took a tiny step back ... and his feet slipped.

Then, like slo-mo in a movie, everything turned into a blur.

Chase tipped backward, splashing down into the water while the guys screamed in agony. The girls could not believe their eyes. A second earlier they were sure Zoey was toast. Now she was the last one standing.

A blast from the air horn made it official. "The girls win the competition!" Mr. Reese yelled.

Removing his helmet, Chase shook the water out of his ears. He wished he could shake loose the last few days along with it. Michael, Dustin, and Logan demanded an explanation. But it was hard to hear them over the cheers of the ecstatic girls.

Quinn, Lola, and Nicole jumped into the pool and swam over to congratulate Zoey. Zoey still could not believe they'd won. She'd thought she was a goner without her baton, and then ...

Still jumping around and screaming with her

teammates, Zoey stole a look at Chase. He looked as stunned as she did.

"How could you do that?" Logan demanded as Michael helped Chase out of the pool. "She had no baton!"

"I slipped," Chase said with a sheepish shrug. It was the only excuse he had. Or at least, it was the only excuse he had for Logan. Michael shot Chase a look. His good friend saw right through him, of course. He knew Chase had fallen on purpose to try and even the score. He only hoped that Zoey knew that, too.

The scene at the after-party was awesome. Cool tunes were pumping from the DJ's table. The buffet was piled high with burgers and lobster and . . . you name it! One thing was certain, Logan's dad knew how to throw a party. So why was Zoey feeling so low? She picked at her lobster. Two seats down, Chase was poking at his plate of food, too.

"How's the lobster?" Chase asked halfheartedly.

Zoey shrugged. "It's fine," she said. She was wearing her favorite new orchid-colored boat-neck top, the one with the sequins. Usually it made her feel great, but not today.

"Good. You know" — Chase gestured toward the

crustacean on Zoey's plate — "they come from the ocean." Zoey gave Chase a look. He was always extra goofy when he was nervous. It wasn't as if she was wondering if lobster were really alien to the planet . . . . "Uh, listen, Zoey . . ." Chase started but trailed off.

Zoey looked him in the face, waiting to hear what he had to say. Chase hesitated. "Yeah?" Zoey prompted.

"Never mind." Chase dropped his hands in his lap. This was incredibly hard.

For a moment they sat in awkward silence. Then Mr. Reese signaled the DJ to turn down the tunes and stood up to make an announcement. "Now, I hope you guys all had a good time these past couple of days," he began. "And congratulations to the girls on their very close victory over the boys."

There were hoots and cheers, and Mr. Reese waited patiently for the cheering to die down. "Now, we have another little surprise for you." He smiled mischievously.

"Before the competition started, we told you the winning team would be on the first episode of *Gender Defenders*," Kira reminded them.

Quinn started to sputter and get red in the face. "What, now you're gonna tell us we won't?" she asked angrily. "'Cause my uncle's a lawyer who —"

"Relax, Quinn." Logan's dad put up his hand. "The girls still get to be on the show. . . . And so do the guys!" he finished with a grin.

"Really?" Michael couldn't believe it.

"We do?" Dustin asked. This was awesome!

"So when do we do it?" Logan wanted to know.

"You've already done it. All the events were taped on hidden camera. Take a look around." Mr. Reese was laughing as he pointed to three different areas. Every place he pointed, a camera operator stepped out from a secret location — by the house, on the roof, even in the bushes — and waved to the kids. They were being filmed the entire time!

The kids were stunned.

"Congratulations, kids. You're gonna be the stars of the very first episode of *Gender Defenders*," Mr. Reese said.

The kids all cheered. Dustin jumped up and down a little higher than usual. Lola and Nicole slapped each other five.

Logan could not believe it. Despite the lameness of their team captain, they were going to be on national TV!

Chase sat in his chair, watching all the commotion. He knew he should be psyched. Stuff like this didn't happen every day. But all he could think about was Zoey. Was their friendship doomed?

After the DJ pressed PLAY and the music started thumping, Chase stole one more look at Zoey. She glanced back at him awkwardly, then looked away.

Chase stared at his hands. He hadn't even told Zoey how he felt and he was experiencing his worst nightmare anyway. Things were never going to be the same again.

CHAPTER 12
Back to School

At PCA, things were almost back to normal when *Gender Defenders* was ready to hit the airwaves.

The Brenner lounge was all abuzz. Guys and girls were gathering to watch *Gender Defenders* — the show's stars included. Lola and Quinn had staked out the prime, front-row beanbag chairs and were not moving.

"How much longer till it comes on?" a girl asked, taking a seat on the couch next to Logan.

"About four more minutes!" Quinn said as she clapped her hands. She could not wait. Everyone and their dog was excited — that is, everyone but Zoey.

Zoey slouched into the girls' lounge and slumped into a chair near Logan's couch. Michael and Nicole came trailing after her.

"C'mon, Zoey, perk up!" Nicole pleaded. It was torture seeing her friend so unhappy. And so unlike Zoey!

"I'm not in a very perkful mood," Zoey grumped. She didn't know if "perkful" was a word or not. But she was sure she was not full of perkiness, and Nicole, as usual, was bubbling over with it.

"But you're about to be on national TV!" Michael pointed out. He wasn't a huge fan of perkiness — but you had to admit it was exciting to be a megastar.

"Yeah." Zoey still didn't sound excited. "Have you guys seen Chase around here yet?" she asked glumly, looking around the packed lounge. She and Chase were still doing the awkward thing, and she was really missing him.

"Yeah," Michael said slowly, shooting a look at Nicole. "He said he's not coming."

"He's not gonna come watch the show with us?" Nicole asked, shocked. She knew things between him and Zoey were weird. But how could he miss this?

Zoey sat up in her chair. "Where is he?" she asked.

Michael shrugged. "He was outside, hangin' by the fountain," he said as he let out his breath.

Now it was Zoey's turn to sigh. Without another word, she got up and left the lounge. Michael and Nicole just watched her go. "Where ya going?" Nicole yelled after her friend.

"The show's about to start!" Michael added. But it was too late. Zoey was gone.

"I'm about to be on TV! I can't believe we're about to be on TV! How cool is that?" Dustin, the blond whirling dervish, zipped into the lounge and bounced off a few walls and a few more people. "Have you ever been on TV?" he asked a random student. "I doubt it! Where you from?" he didn't pause for the girl to answer. His Frazz was still juicing him up, and he could not seem to stop talking. "My name's Dustin! I'm about to be on TV!"

"Okay, when is your Frazz going to wear off?" Lola asked Quinn, watching the Frazz Spaz from her seat.

"I don't know," Quinn answered. She looked really worried. She might have been able to take a guess but suddenly Dustin was hanging over her shoulder, talking a mile a minute.

"Can you believe we're gonna be on TV? Y'know, the best part about being on TV is that —"

Suddenly Dustin went from sixty to zero. He collapsed across Quinn's lap and lay there, facedown, silent and not moving. He was passed out cold.

Quinn looked at Lola. Finally! "It wore off," she announced with relief.

Truth Be Told

Chase sat on the edge of the fountain, tapping his sneakers and staring at the ocean in the distance. He wished he could turn back time and make things okay with Zoey again. But he couldn't. All he could do was wait and hope.

Zoey walked up behind Chase, stopped in front of him, and waited.

"Uh . . . you wanna sit down?" he asked, taking his foot off the fountain wall.

"Okay." Zoey climbed up and flipped her hair out of her face. She looked stellar in a blue print tank top, low-rise jeans, big earrings, and a cool belt.

"Look," Chase started. He knew it was now or never. He needed to come clean with Zoey, pronto. He'd already lost her friendship — he had little more to lose. Still, it was hard. "The reason . . . the reason I took your

TekMate . . . was that . . . I wrote a text message to Michael . . . and I sent it to you by mistake."

Zoey just listened. So Chase kept going.

"And I had to get your TekMate away from you so I could erase the message before you read it," Chase explained. "I tried to put it back, but you ran off, so I couldn't."

"Okay," Zoey said, nodding.

"Do you believe me?" Chase asked.

"Should I not?" Zoey asked aloud. What Chase said to her on the patio at Logan's was true. She did know he was an honest guy — at least until recently. He had never given her a reason to think otherwise.

"No, you should," Chase assured her.

"Then I do," Zoey confirmed.

"Okay." Chase hoped they were through, but his explanation left one big question unanswered.

Zoey wanted that answer. "So . . ." she began.

"Don't ask," Chase begged, interrupting her.

"I'm asking."

"Zoey, don't —" They were so close to being friends again, Chase didn't want to start this whole thing all over.

Zoey couldn't let it go. "What was the message you sent me by mistake? Tell me."

"I'd really rather not tell you." Chase shook his head.

"Why, was it mean?" Zoey squinched her eyebrows. She couldn't imagine Chase being mean. She really couldn't imagine what he had to hide from her, either.

"Huh?" Chase was stunned. "Mean?"

"Did you say something mean about me?" Zoey asked again.

"No! No, no, it was nothing like that. I'd never say anything mean about you." Chase was flustered. It was the exact opposite.

"Then what could you have written that was so important to hide from me? What was the message?"

"You really wanna know?" Chase cringed. He couldn't have Zoey thinking he said something mean. He had to tell her.

"Yeah."

"You're sure?" Chase asked, hoping she might change her mind.

"I really wanna know," Zoey insisted.

"Okay. The message was —"

"Guys!" Nicole, Michael, Logan, and Lola came running up to them full tilt. Chase rolled his eyes. He was finally ready to tell Zoey everything — if they could only have a minute alone.

"Guys, the show's starting in, like, thirty seconds!" Logan said, tapping his huge watch.

"We're not letting you miss this!" Michael insisted.

"C'mon! We're gonna be on TV!" Nicole grabbed Zoey's arm and yanked her back toward Brenner. Lola and Logan were on Chase. The whole gang ran all the way to the lounge and made it as the opening credits began to roll.

From the side of the room Chase could not tear his eyes off of Zoey. She smiled at him, then turned back to the show.

Chase was lost in thought. Michael's voice echoed in his head. "Just tell Zoey you love her." How many times had his best friend told him to do it? Maybe it wasn't such bad advice.

Slipping his TekMate off of his hip, Chase typed: "The message was . . . I LOVE YOU."

Then, before he could change his mind, Chase took a deep breath and pressed SEND. He snapped his TekMate closed and slid it into his holster. The kids were going nuts in the lounge. The show was a total hit! Chase couldn't hear a thing. He waited and watched, wanting to see Zoey go for her TekMate. Shouldn't it be beeping or vibrating by now?

The seconds seemed like years. What was taking so

long? Chase looked closer. Zoey had her TekMate holder on, but the strap was unclipped, and her TekMate was gone! Suddenly Chase felt ill. He'd finally gotten up the nerve to tell Zoey the truth, and her TekMate was nowhere to be seen! Where the heck was it?

Back on the fountain wall, a lonely pink TekMate vibrated closer and closer to the edge of the water. On the screen a message flashed. A message Zoey would never get. The TekMate wiggled its way over the edge and slipped into the water. The words I LOVE YOU flashed for one more moment, and the screen went dark.